The Grumpy Tree

Written and Illustrated
by
Leo Price

Pauline
BOOKS & MEDIA
BOSTON

Library of Congress Cataloging-in-Publication Data

Price, Leo.
   [Tree that always said no!]
   The grumpy tree / written and illustrated by Leo Price.
      p. cm.
   Summary: An unfriendly tree in the forest learns the value of having helpful friends.
   ISBN 0-8198-3097-6
   [1. Friendship Fiction.   2. Trees Fiction   3. Animals Fiction   4. Conduct of life Fiction.]
   I. Title.
PZ7.P9307Gr   1999
[E]—dc21   99–26651
                                                CIP

**Dedicated to
Rev. Donald Ricard
and his family,
in gratitude for their help**

Printed in Korea. Published in the U.S.A. by Pauline Books & Media, 50 Saint Pauls Avenue, Boston, MA 02130-3491.

www.pauline.org

Pauline Books & Media is the publishing house of the Daughters of St. Paul, an international congregation of women religious serving the Church with the communications media.

1 2 3 4 5 6   05 04 03 02 01 00

In the center of the green forest lived a tall Tree. He knew he was shady and cool. He thought of himself as the best tree in the whole forest.

One day two squirrels came searching for a home. "Oh, what a wonderful tree!" Mrs. Squirrel exclaimed.

"It's perfect!" agreed Mr. Squirrel.

"You down there!" the Tree roared. "What do you think you're doing?"

"We were thinking of making you our new home."

"No! I can't be bothered!"

"But we won't be any bother," Mrs. Squirrel said politely. "We are very well-mannered."

"Besides, your shiny green leaves and lofty branches will make a perfect home," added Mr. Squirrel.

"Flattery doesn't impress me," replied the Tree. "I won't share with you or with anyone else!"

"What a shame," sighed Mr. Squirrel. "We'll never find a better tree."

Discouraged, the squirrels walked off through the forest.

"Finally some peace and quiet," the Tree said with a big yawn. "I'm so sleepy."

At that moment Little Bear walked by. Now Little Bear was always looking for something sweet to eat.

My, what a lovely tree! he thought. *Just the place to find some bees and honey! I think I'll take a look while he's sleeping.*

"Hey, Bear! Where are you going?" the Tree suddenly shouted. "You may not realize it, but you have very sharp claws. And one of them happens to be sticking in my ear!"

"I'm very sorry," apologized Little Bear. "It's just that I was hoping to find some bees and honey. I thought for sure you'd have some. Ooh...when I think of finding bees and honey, I sometimes forget myself!"

I don't care what you want!" roared the Tree.
"And even if I had any honey in one of my hollow
branches, I wouldn't share it with you!"

8

A tree like you is not sweet enough to have honey, thought Little Bear. But just as he was about to turn around and climb down, the Tree called: "Come down this instant, or I'll shake you down!"

And with that, the Tree began to rattle his branches and shake his trunk, until Little Bear slipped off and tumbled to the forest floor. He barely missed hitting the Tree's big nose as he fell.

The Tree frowned down on Little Bear.

"You have no right to climb my branches. Don't you understand? I don't want to share with you or with anyone else!"

"Oh, how it hurts!" Little Bear moaned, as he limped away. "Why is that Tree so grumpy? One thing's for sure, I'll never climb again without asking!"

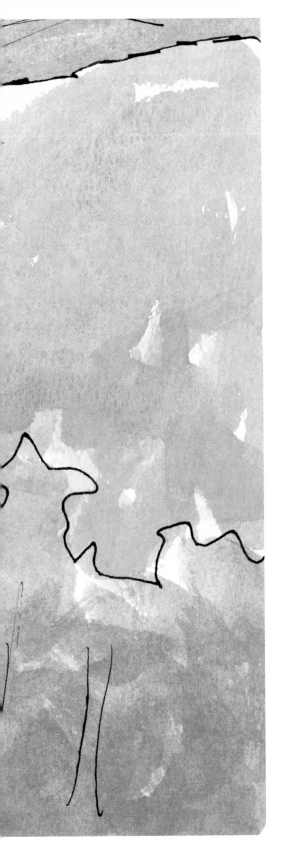

No sooner had Little Bear left, than a tiny bird came and landed on the Tree's nose. It was very tired.

"Tweet! Tweet! Tweet!" it chirped. "Here's the perfect spot for a little rest!"

To the bird's surprise, two mossy eyes were glaring at him. "What are YOU doing here?" the Tree demanded.

"Oh! Good day to you, too, friend Tree!"

I find it rather difficult to breathe, friend Bird, with you perched upon my nose!"

"But I'm really not that heavy, Mr. Tree. Perhaps you don't want to talk and be friendly. I guess I'll just leave you to yourself."

And off the tired bird flew, barely having had time to catch his breath.

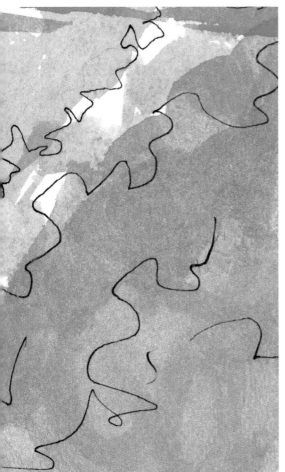

Well, thought the Tree, *that takes care of that!*

From then on, it was as though some quiet voice had told all the creatures of the forest to leave the grumpy Tree alone.

For the longest time, the Tree saw no one. He heard no one. He was left all alone. The grumpy Tree actually began to feel a little lonely.

Just as he was feeling sorry for himself, the Tree felt a strange tickle—first on his long nose, then all over his trunk! "Who are you, if I might ask?" he inquired.

"No tree wants to be our friend. They just want our stay to end. But our favorite snack is tree. We're the termite family!"

ermites! Get out of my branches and off of my trunk, or I'll shake you off! I won't share with you or with anyone else!"

"You can shake both night and day, but, sweet Tree, we're here to stay!"

"WHAT?! No way! Get off! Get off, I said! Right NOW!"

The Tree gathered his roots under him for the mightiest shake he had ever shaken. The ground trembled! The bark flew! The Tree shook and shook. But not one termite fell.

For the first time, the Tree felt helpless. And he began to cry.

The termites really meant to stay. And termites always make holes in wood. The holes would hurt the Tree and keep him from being the best tree he could be.

And once the termites made many, many holes, the Tree would come crashing down!

"O-o-o-oh, what will I do?" he sobbed.

Just then, Little Bear, who had been treated so unkindly by the Tree, popped out of the bushes. Little Bear still remembered the Tree's grumpiness. But he wanted to be friendly, so he asked what the trouble was.

O h, Little Bear, can you see how these termites are eating away at me? I'm afraid that I'll never be myself again!"

"This seems serious!" declared Little Bear. "I'm not sure what I can do to help, because I've never had termites. But I have a good friend who might know what to do. She's awfully wise. I'll be right back!"

And so the bear ran off to find his friend.

"Hello! Mrs. Owl, are you home?"

"Yes. I'm up here! It's good to see you, my friend, it's just that this bright sunlight hurts my eyes."

"Do you remember the Tree in the middle of the forest?" Little Bear asked. "The one who was so unkind to me?"

You mean the grumpy Tree, the one who never shares with anyone?"

"That's him, and he's in trouble. Can you come and help?"

"Of course! Let's go!"

Since the Tree had become the home of termites, Mrs. Owl told Little Bear that there was not a moment to lose. And off they went to the middle of the forest.

"W-h-o-o! This doesn't look good!" Mrs. Owl exclaimed when she saw the Tree. "Go and get the Woodpecker Family—and hurry!"

"I'm on my way!" cried Little Bear.

The Woodpecker Family
knew the Tree of whom
Little Bear spoke. The Tree had
not shared with them when
they wanted to look for grubs
under his bark. But they
wanted to be friendly, too. And
so they went with Little Bear.

Not a minute was wasted. The woodpeckers knew exactly what to do about termites.

Soon the forest was filled with the sounds of busy beaks.

"Wow! Look at those termites go!" exclaimed Little Bear. "It's incredible!"

The tree could hardly believe how wonderful he felt!

"I'm so glad you're better!" Little Bear called as he waved good-bye.

Please wait, Little Bear!" the Tree cried out. "And Mrs. Owl and the Woodpecker Family too! Let me thank you! I never knew what it meant to have a friend... someone who understands and cares about me. Could I be your friend from now on?"

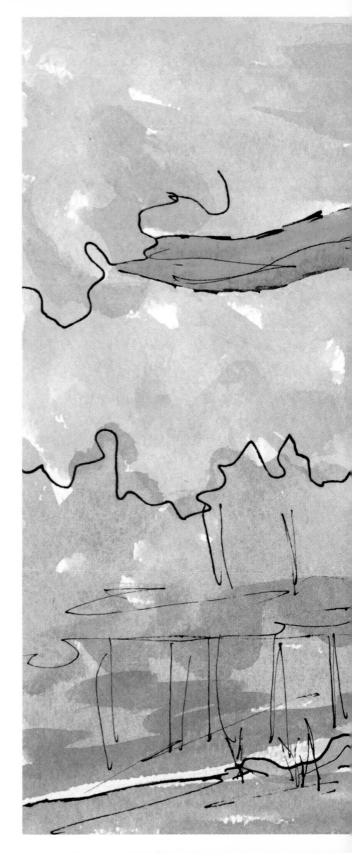

Yes! Hooray! Hooray!" the animals shouted.

And so the Tree discovered what true friendship meant. He had never been so happy!

From that time on, the Tree learned to share. He enjoyed spending time with all his friends, especially with Little Bear, who loved to go hunting for honey in the Tree's broad branches.

And soon enough, instead of being known as the grumpy Tree, the Tree became known as the *friendliest* tree in the forest. That was something he liked far, far better.

For Parents and Teachers

The Grumpy Tree highlights three main themes: forgiveness/reconciliation, sharing and friendship.

Here are some discussion questions which you might wish to use with your child or children after reading the story together.

Forgiveness and reconciliation

- Was the Tree very nice to the animals at the beginning of the story? What were some of the things the Tree said or did to the animals?
- Even though the Tree was grumpy and unkind, did the animals try to "get even" with him by being mean themselves? How can we tell that Little Bear, Mrs. Owl and the Woodpecker Family forgave the Tree for being grumpy and refusing to share?
- Is it always easy to forgive and to be kind to someone who has hurt us?
- What was special about the way Little Bear and the other animals helped the grumpy Tree? (Hint: Did they think they would get something out of it?)
- What did the grumpy Tree do after the animals saved him from the termites? Was he grumpy anymore?
- The Tree had been grumpy because he had never had any friends. Sometimes people we know may act in a grumpy way because they are hurt or lonely. What can we do to help people like this?

Sharing

- The animals in the story hoped that the Tree would share the good things he had with them. Can you remember and name some of these things?
- How did the animals feel when the grumpy Tree wouldn't share? Did anyone ever tell you they wouldn't share with you? How did that make you feel?
- What are some things that you have and can share with others? (After some answers are offered, continue with....) What are some other very special things that only *you* can share? (Hint: Your love, your smile, etc.)
- Is it always easy to share? Why?

- Can you remember the last time you shared something with someone? How did you feel after you shared?

Friendship

- Do you like having friends? Why?
- How do you show that you are friends with someone?
- How was the Tree in the story unfriendly toward the animals? What made him finally change and become friendly?
- Is it always easy to get along with your friends? What was something Little Bear did in the story that made it easier for him to become the grumpy Tree's friend? (Hint: Try to prompt your child (children) to realize that forgiveness is a very important part of friendship.)
- Have you ever been unfriendly or grumpy with someone? What did you feel like when you were grumpy? How did your grumpiness go away?
- Were you happy when the Tree decided to make friends at the end of the story? Why?

BOOKS & MEDIA

The Daughters of St. Paul operate book and media centers at the following addresses. Visit, call or write the one nearest you today, or find us on the World Wide Web, www.pauline.org

CALIFORNIA
3908 Sepulveda Blvd., Culver City, CA 90230   310-397-8676
5945 Balboa Ave., San Diego, CA 92111   619-565-9181
46 Geary Street, San Francisco, CA 94108   415-781-5180
FLORIDA
145 S.W. 107th Ave., Miami, FL 33174   305-559-6715
HAWAII
1143 Bishop Street, Honolulu, HI 96813   808-521-2731
Neighbor Islands call: 800-259-8463
ILLINOIS
172 North Michigan Ave., Chicago, IL 60601   312-346-4228
LOUISIANA
4403 Veterans Memorial Blvd., Metairie, LA 70006   504-887-7631
MASSACHUSETTS
Rte. 1, 885 Providence Hwy., Dedham, MA 02026   781-326-5385
MISSOURI
9804 Watson Rd., St. Louis, MO 63126   314-965-3512
NEW JERSEY
561 U.S. Route 1, Wick Plaza, Edison, NJ 08817   732-572-1200
NEW YORK
150 East 52nd Street, New York, NY 10022   212-754-1110
78 Fort Place, Staten Island, NY 10301   718-447-5071
OHIO
2105 Ontario Street (at Prospect Ave.), Cleveland, OH 44115   216-621-9427
PENNSYLVANIA
9171-A Roosevelt Blvd., Philadelphia, PA 19114   215-676-9494
SOUTH CAROLINA
243 King Street, Charleston, SC 29401   843-577-0175
TENNESSEE
4811 Poplar Ave., Memphis, TN 38117   901-761-2987
TEXAS
114 Main Plaza, San Antonio, TX 78205   210-224-8101
VIRGINIA
1025 King Street, Alexandria, VA 22314   703-549-3806
CANADA
3022 Dufferin Street, Toronto, Ontario, Canada M6B 3T5   416-781-9131
1155 Yonge Street, Toronto, Ontario, Canada M4T 1W2   416-934-3440

¡También somos su fuente para libros, videos y música en español!